FUNNY JOKES

FOR

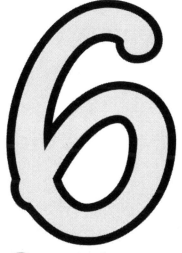

YEAR OLD KIDS

HUNDREDS OF HILARIOUS JOKES INSIDE!

JIMMY JONES

Hundreds of really funny, hilarious jokes that will have the kids in fits of laughter in no time!

They're all in here - the funniest
- Jokes
- Riddles
- Tongue Twisters
- Knock Knock Jokes

for 6 year old kids!

Funny kids love funny jokes and this brand new collection of original and classic jokes promises hours of fun for the whole family!

Books by Jimmy Jones

Funny Jokes For Funny Kids
Knock Knock Jokes For Funny Kids

Funny Jokes For Kids Series
All Ages 5 -12!

To see all the latest books by
Jimmy Jones just go to
kidsjokebooks.com

Contents

Funny Jokes!

What is a sailor's favorite lunch?
Fish and ships!

Why didn't the bear wear shoes to school?
He liked to have bear feet!

Where do rabbits go after they get married?
On their Bunnymoon!

Why did Mickey Mouse join NASA?
He wanted to visit Pluto!

What did the Cinderella penguin wear to the ball?
Glass flippers!

Why was the glow worm looking sad?
Her kids weren't very bright!

Why did the butterfly leave the dance?
It was a moth ball!

What do you call a snowman who has been sunbaking for a week?
Water!

How do you get a spaceman's baby to sleep?
Rocket!

What did the magic tractor do last Saturday?
Turned into a corn field!

What do you call a boy on the stage?
Mike!

What did the taxi driver say to the frog?
Hop in!

Why didn't the girl like the pizza joke?
It was way too cheesy!

Why did the fish live in salt water?
Pepper made him sneeze!

Where did the dog park his car?
The Barking Lot!

No matter how many times you try, which word is always spelt wrong?

Wrong!

How do you fit lots more pigs on your farm?

Build a huge sty-scraper!

Where do computers party all night?

The Disk O!

What goes up if the rain comes down?
An umbrella!

How can you tell if a vampire is getting a cold?
By his loud coffin!

What do you call a grumpy cow?
MOOOO-dy!

Why was the detective duck given the key to the city?

He quacked the case!

What did the chewing gum say to the shoe?

Let's stick together!

What has 4 legs, a trunk and wears sunglasses?

A mouse on holiday!

Why did the lady wear a helmet to dinner?
She was on a crash diet!

What do you call an adult bear that has no teeth?
The gummy bear!

How do you stop a dog from digging holes in your back yard?
Put him in the front yard!

What kind of cat is no fun to play a game with?

The cheetah!

What do you call a football playing cat?

Puss in boots!

Why did the scarecrow get a big pay rise?

He was a leader in his field!

Why are ghosts no good at lying?
You can usually see right through them!

Why did the whale learn to play the trumpet?
So he could join the Orca-Stra!

Why did the toilet paper roll down the steep hill?
He wanted to get to the bottom!

What is white and black and eats like a horse?

A zebra!

What did the hamburger name his daughter?

Patty!

What fruit do vampires love?

Necktarines!

What does a frog like to drink with his dinner?

Croak-a-cola!

What is orange, grows in the ground and sounds like a parrot?

A carrot!

What happens when 2 silkworms have a race?

It ends in a tie!

What do you call a great florist?
Blossom!

What's the proper name for a camel with 3 humps?
Humphrey!

What do you call a boy in your hot tub?
Stew!

What did the toilet roll say to the toilet?
You're looking a bit flushed!

What was the witch's favorite subject at witch school?
Spelling!

What do you call a rodeo rider?
Buck!

Where do all polar bears go to vote?
The North Poll!

What did the picture say to the window?
Help! I've been framed!

What do you call a frog sitting on a chair?
A toadstool!

What do you get if you dive into the Red Sea?

Wet!

Where do fish keep their spare cash?

The river bank!

There were 4 cats on a chair and one jumped off. How many were left?

None, because they were copycats!

What do you call a man who lives in the toilet?

John!

What is the best cure for dandruff?

Going bald!

Why did the cows all go to Broadway?

To see the mooosicals!

Why did the witch itch?
She lost her W!

What do you call a witch who lives near the beach?
A sandwitch!

Why do tigers eat raw meat?
They never learned to cook!

Which bird should wear a wig?
The bald eagle!

What did the crab say to the big wave?
Long time no sea!

When is it bad luck if a black cat follows you?
When you are a grey mouse!

Why didn't the boy like the wooden car with the wooden engine.

It wooden go!

Why are tennis players so loud?

They always raise a racquet!

Why do bees hum?

They don't know the words!

What is the key to a great space party?
Always planet early!

What did the snowman eat for his breakfast?
Frosted Flakes!

What is a cat's favorite car?
CAT-illacs!

What kind of key will never unlock a door?
A monkey!

Which bird steals soap from the bathtub?
The robber duck!

Why don't pigs play football?
They hog the ball!

Why did the bowling pins fall over?
They were on strike!

What do you get if an elephant stands on the roof of your house?
Mushed rooms!

What has one horn and lots of milk?
A milk truck!

What kind of sandwich did the shark order for his lunch?

Peanut butter and jellyfish!

What did the potato chip say to the biscuit?

Let's go for a dip!

How did the rabbit get to another city?

By hare plane!

What goes up and then down but doesn't
actually move?
Stairs!

Why did the teacher go to the pool?
To test the water!

What do you call a boy on your doorstep?
Matt!

Where is the witch's garage?
The broom closet!

Why was the broom late for work at the factory?
He overswept!

What was the fly doing in the bowl of soup?
Backstroke!

How do birds learn to fly for the very first time?

They wing it!

What do you call a snake that has no clothes on?

Snaked!

What is the busiest time to go to the dentist?

Tooth hurty! (2.30)

Why did the boy stand on a cow?
To be a cowboy!

Where do chickens go for a laugh?
The funny farm!

If a lion ate a clown how would he feel?
A bit funny!

Funny Knock Knock Jokes!

Knock knock.

Who's there?

X.

X who?

X on toast for breakfast? Great idea!

Knock knock.

Who's there?

Fangs.

Fangs who?

Fangs for letting me come to your party. It's gonna be fun!

Knock knock.

Who's there?

Emma.

Emma who?

Emma very hungry!

What's for dinner?

Knock knock.

Who's there?

Noah.

Noah who?

Noah good place for lunch?

How about pizza?

Knock knock.

Who's there?

Riot.

Riot who?

I'm Riot on time so let's go!

Knock knock.

Who's there?

Leaf.

Leaf who?

Leaf the key under the mat next time!

Knock knock.

Who's there?

Max.

Max who?

Max no difference to me as I can't remember my last name!

Knock knock.

Who's there?

Cheese.

Cheese who?

For cheese a jolly good fellow, for cheese a jolly good fellow!

Knock knock.

Who's there?

Fork.

Fork who?

Fork got to mention, why is your doorbell broken?

Knock knock.

Who's there?

Leah.

Leah who?

Leah the door unlocked next time, and then I won't have to knock!

Knock knock.

Who's there?

Lego.

Lego who?

Lego of the handle so I can open this door!

Knock knock.

Who's there?

Terrain.

Terrain who?

It's starting terrain, do you have an umbrella?

Knock knock.

Who's there?

Claire.

Claire who?

Claire the way!

Skateboarder coming through!

Knock knock.

Who's there?

Candice.

Candice who?

Candice door open any quicker

please?

Knock knock.

Who's there?

Jimmy.

Jimmy who?

Jimmy 2 seconds and I will tell you

all about it!

Knock knock.

Who's there?

Phillip.

Phillip who?

Phillip your pool so we can swim!

Knock knock.

Who's there?

I am.

I am who?

Actually you are you!

Knock knock.

Who's there?

Scold.

Scold who?

Scold enough today to make a snowman!

Knock knock.

Who's there?

Garden.

Garden who?

Garden the treasure chest from the pirates. Aarrrrrr!

Knock knock.

Who's there?

Frank.

Frank who?

Frank ly speaking I would really like it if you fixed your doorbell!

Knock knock.

Who's there?

Todd.

Todd who?

Todd ay is the your lucky day because I am here!

Knock knock.

Who's there?

Irish.

Irish who?

Irish you could come to my place for dinner. Mom's making pizza!

Knock knock.

Who's there?

Howard.

Howard who?

Howard you like to go to the park and play ball?

Knock knock.

Who's there?

Jess.

Jess who?

Jess let me in please! It's cold out here!

Knock knock.

Who's there?

Waiter.

Waiter who?

Waiter I finish telling all these jokes!

Then I'll tell you some more!

Knock knock.

Who's there?

Dora.

Dora who?

Dora's locked so should I climb

through the window?

Knock knock.

Who's there?

Bean.

Bean who?

Bean waiting here for ages!

Why are you always late?

Knock knock.

Who's there?

Hada.

Hada who?

Hada great weekend, how about you?

Knock knock.

Who's there?

Dozen.

Dozen who?

Dozen anybody want to let me in?

It's cold out here!

Knock knock.

Who's there?

Loaf.

Loaf who?

I loaf pizza! Do you want some?

Knock knock.

Who's there?

Kim.

Kim who?

Kim here and give me a kiss!

I have missed you so much!

Knock knock.

Who's there?

Police.

Police who?

Police hurry up and open this door!

Knock knock.

Who's there?

Wire.

Wire who?

Wire we talking through this door?

Open up already!

Knock knock.

Who's there?

Turnip.

Turnip who?

Turnip the music! It's time to party!

Knock knock.

Who's there?

Freddy.

Freddy who?

Freddy set, go!

I'll race you to the letterbox!

Knock knock.

Who's there?

Kanye.

Kanye who?

Kanye please open this door before it

starts to rain!

Knock knock.

Who's there?

Ken.

Ken who?

Ken I please have a drink?

I am so thirsty!

Knock knock.

Who's there?

Anne.

Anne who?

Anne imals are fun so let's go to the

zoo and play with the baby tigers!

Knock knock.

Who's there?

Al.

Al who?

Al tell you if you open this door and

let me in!

Knock knock.

Who's there?

Icing.

Icing who?

Icing many songs. Which one would

you like to hear?

Knock knock.

Who's there?

Hugo.

Hugo who?

Hugo where I go and I go where Hugo!

Knock knock.

Who's there?

Ida.

Ida who?

Ida like to speak with you about our new range of doorbells!

Knock knock.

Who's there?

Flea.

Flea who?

I knocked Flea times! Why didn't you answer?

Knock knock.

Who's there?

Zany.

Zany who?

Zany body home today? Let me in!

Knock knock.

Who's there?

Earl.

Earl who?

Earl be very happy when you let me in!

Knock knock.

Who's there?

Mikey.

Mikey who?

Mikey is too big for the keyhole!

Noooooo!

Knock knock.

Who's there?

Figs.

Figs who?

Figs the bell please, this knocking is so last year!

Knock knock.

Who's there?

Honey bee.

Honey bee who?

Honey bee kind and open the door for your grandma!

Knock knock.

Who's there?

Teresa.

Teresa who?

Teresa very green this time of year!

Knock knock.

Who's there?

Kanga.

Kanga who?

No, kangaroo!

Knock knock.

Who's there?

Iona.

Iona who?

Iona brand new car! Come and see!

Knock knock.

Who's there?

Mushroom.

Mushroom who?

There wasn't mushroom at the party so I left!

Knock knock.

Who's there?

Tank.

Tank who?

You're very welcome madam!

Knock knock.

Who's there?

Alpaca.

Alpaca who?

Alpaca my bags in the morning and be on my way!

Knock knock.

Who's there?

Troy.

Troy who?

Troy to answer quicker next time please!

Knock knock.

Who's there?

Beth.

Beth who?

Beth friends stick together so let's go!

Knock knock.

Who's there?

Locky.

Locky who?

Locky I caught you before you went out!

Knock knock.

Who's there?

Barbara.

Barbara who?

Barbara black sheep, have you any wool?

Knock knock.

Who's there?

Athena.

Athena who?

Athena bear in your house so RUN!!!!!

Knock knock.

Who's there?

Soda.

Soda who?

Soda you want to let me in or what?

Funny Riddles!

What starts working when it is fired?
A rocket!

What has 4 legs but no tail?
A frog!

What holds water but has many holes?
A sponge!

What runs all day but never moves?
Your refrigerator!

What can you draw without a pencil?
The blinds!

What is there more of the less you see?
Darkness!

What has a head and a tail but no arms?
A coin!

What has a head, a tail, is brown and has no legs?
A Penny!

Which bee will never sting you?
A frisbee!

What goes up and down but doesn't move?
Stairs!

What has 2 legs but can't walk?
A pair of jeans!

What has many limbs but cannot walk?
A tree!

What has an eye but cannot see?
A hurricane!

What can you touch but never see?
Your back!

What has feet on the inside but not the outside?
Shoes!

What can you measure even though sometimes it flies?

Time!

What can you hold without touching it?

Your breath!

What is always coming but never arrives?

Tomorrow!

What kind of bow is very hard to tie?
A rainbow!

What has many keys but can't open a door?
A piano!

What kind of room has no windows or doors?
A mushroom!

What is always taken before you get it?
Your photo!

What is thin, can bend, is red on the inside with a nail on the end?
A finger!

How do you make seven an even number?
Take away the S!

What flies all day but doesn't move far?
A flag!

How many apples can you put into an empty bag?
One. Now it's not empty!

What runs around a field but never moves?
A fence!

Which ring is always square?
A boxing ring!

What is black and white and red all over?
A newspaper!

Which water can you chew and eat?
Watermelon!

What has eyes but cannot see?
A potato!

I have branches but no leaves. What am I?
A bank!

What is black and white, black and white?
A penguin rolling down a hill!

What does everyone have but never lose?
Their shadow!

What gets bigger the more you take away
from it?
A hole!

When does B come after U?
When you take its honey!

Funny Tongue Twisters!

Tongue Twisters are great fun!
Start off slow.
How fast can you go?

Butter brown bread.
Butter brown bread.
Butter brown bread.

Which witch wishes.
Which witch wishes.
Which witch wishes.

Dog chews shoes.
Dog chews shoes.
Dog chews shoes.

Fred fed Ted bread.
Fred fed Ted bread.
Fred fed Ted bread.

Red lolly, yellow lolly.
Red lolly, yellow lolly.
Red lolly, yellow lolly.

She sees cheese.
She sees cheese.
She sees cheese.

Free fluffy feathers.
Free fluffy feathers.
Free fluffy feathers.

Cranky cat classes.
Cranky cat classes.
Cranky cat classes.

Five free flying frogs.
Five free flying frogs.
Five free flying frogs.

Lick yellow lollies.
Lick yellow lollies.
Lick yellow lollies.

Three flies feed.
Three flies feed.
Three flies feed.

Dad draws dogs.
Dad draws dogs.
Dad draws dogs.

The fish shop sells shellfish.
The fish shop sells shellfish.
The fish shop sells shellfish.

Big blue bug.
Big blue bug.
Big blue bug.

Fred's flag flew fast.
Fred's flag flew fast.
Fred's flag flew fast.

Susan's shoe shine shop.
Susan's shoe shine shop.
Susan's shoe shine shop.

The selfish elf ate shellfish.
The selfish elf ate shellfish.
The selfish elf ate shellfish.

Tommy Tucker tried ties.
Tommy Tucker tried ties.
Tommy Tucker tried ties.

Grey goats graze.
Grey goats graze.
Grey goats graze.

Six slippery snails slide.
Six slippery snails slide.
Six slippery snails slide.

Green glass globes.
Green glass globes.
Green glass globes.

Bob's blue balloons.
Bob's blue balloons.
Bob's blue balloons.

Six sick sheep.
Six sick sheep.
Six sick sheep.

Bonus Funny Jokes!

What kind of car did the cat drive to work?
A Cattilac!

What did the 2 cats do after a fight?
Hiss and make up!

Why did the strawberry look so sad?
It was a blue berry!

Which day of the week is the hottest?
Sun-day!

What do you call a girl who loves honey?
Bea!

What fish would never bite a woman?
A man eating shark!

How do snowmen learn things?
They go on the winternet!

Why was the spider hanging out on the computer?
He was making a website!

What does every winner lose in a race?
Their breath!

What did the dad potato name his son?
Chip!

What do you call a girl who likes to cook outside?
Barbie!

What do you call a lion that likes to wear top hats?
A dandy lion!

What is an alligator's favorite sports drink?
GatorAde!

What do you call a boy stuck to the wall?
Art!

What do fish like to watch on TV?
Whale of Fortune!

What do you call a dog with a sore throat?
A husky!

What did the lazy dog do for fun?
Chase a parked car!

What roads do ghosts like to haunt?
Dead ends!

What is a small dog's favorite type of pizza?
Pupparoni!

Why wouldn't the oyster share her pearls?
She was a little shellfish!

What was in the scary ghost's nose?
Boooogers!

What did the crab take when it was sick?
Vitamin sea!

What kind of flower is on your dad's face?
Tulips!

Why did Humpty Dumpty love autumn so much?
He had a great fall!

What do you call a boy named Lee sitting by himself?

Lonely! (Lone Lee)

How can you make friends with a squirrel?

Climb up a tree and act like a nut!

What is a cat's favorite color?

PURRRRR_ple!

Which bet has never been won?
The alphabet!

Why was the oak tree at the dentist?
It was having a root canal!

How do hair stylists do haircuts faster?
They take short cuts!

What did the traffic light say to the school bus?

Don't look, I'm changing!

What was the alligator's favorite game?

Snap!

What did the baby corn ask his mother?

Where is pop corn?

What did the elephant say to her naughty children?

Tusk Tusk!

What do you call the girl who has a frog on her head?

Lily!

What's the cheapest way to buy an elephant?

At a jumbo sale!

Bonus

Knock Knock Jokes!

Knock knock.

Who's there?

Wire.

Wire who?

Wire you still inside? Let's go!

Knock knock.

Who's there?

Toucan.

Toucan who?

Toucan play that sort of game!

Knock knock.

Who's there?

Lettuce.

Lettuce who?

Please lettuce in before our ice cream melts!

Knock knock.

Who's there?

Will.

Will who?

Will you marry me?

Knock knock.

Who's there?

Stopwatch.

Stopwatch who?

Stopwatch you're doing and let me in!

Knock knock.

Who's there?

Sadie.

Sadie who?

Sadie magic word and your wish will come true!

Knock knock.

Who's there?

Luke.

Luke who?

Luke through the window and find out!

Knock knock.

Who's there?

Voodoo.

Voodoo who?

Voodoo you think it is knocking?

Santa Claus?

Knock knock.

Who's there?

Boo.

Boo who?

It's not that sad!

Pull yourself together!

Knock knock.

Who's there?

Nose.

Nose who?

I Nose plenty more Knock knock

jokes for you!

Knock knock.

Who's there?

Annie.

Annie who?

Annie body home?

I've bought you a present!

Knock knock.

Who's there?

Justin.

Justin who?

Justin case you didn't know, it's going to rain in a minute!

Knock knock.

Who's there?

Window.

Window who?

Window you have time to come over

to my house?

Knock knock.

Who's there?

Aloha.

Aloha who?

Aloha bell would be handy because

then I could reach it!

Knock knock.

Who's there?

Ariel.

Ariel who?

Ariel lly want to come inside so let me in already!

Knock knock.

Who's there?

Fiddle.

Fiddle who?

Fiddle make you happy I'll keep telling jokes!

Knock knock.

Who's there?

Peas.

Peas who?

Peas let me in! I really need to use the bathroom! It's an emergency!

Knock knock.

Who's there?

Henrietta.

Henrietta who?

Henrietta apple and he found half a worm!

Knock knock.

Who's there?

Hannah.

Hannah who?

Hannah one and a two and a three and a four!

Knock knock.

Who's there?

Java.

Java who?

Java cup of sugar for my mom?

Knock knock.

Who's there?

Grub.

Grub who?

Grub hold of my hand and I will show you the way!

Knock knock.

Who's there?

Lena.

Lena who?

Lena bit closer and I'll tell you all about it!

Knock knock.

Who's there?

Fanny.

Fanny who?

Fanny body home?

Why don't you answer?

Knock knock.

Who's there?

Harry.

Harry who?

Harry up! It's so cold a penguin

would freeze!

Thank you so much

For reading our book.

I hope you have enjoyed these funny jokes for 6 year old kids as much as my kids and I did as we were putting this book together.

We really had a lot of fun and laughter creating and compiling this book and we really appreciate you for reading our book.

If you could possibly let us know what you thought of our book by way of a review we would really appreciate it 😊

To see all our latest books or leave a review just go to
kidsjokebooks.com
Once again, thanks so much for reading.

All the best,
Jimmy Jones
And also Ella & Alex (the kids)
And even Obi (the dog – he's very cute!)

Made in the USA
San Bernardino, CA
30 November 2019